BARBARA WILLIAMS

The Horrible, Impossible, Bad Witch Child

ILLUSTRATED BY CAROL NICKLAUS

AN AVON CAMELOT BOOK

THE HORRIBLE, IMPOSSIBLE BAD WITCH CHILD is an original publication of Avon Books. This work has never before appeared in book form.

3rd grade reading level has been determined by using the Fry Readability Scale.

AVON BOOKS
A division of
The Hearst Corporation
959 Eighth Avenue
New York, New York 10019

Published by arrangement with the author
Library of Congress Catalog Card Number: 81-70558
ISBN: 0-380-80283-x

Library of Congress Cataloging in Publication Data

Williams, Barbara.
  The horrible, impossible bad witch child.

  (A Snuggle & read story book) (An Avon/Camelot
book)
  Summary: A nasty little witch girl is transformed
into a beautiful princess by a magical frog.
  [1. Witches—Fiction.   2. Magic—Fiction]
I. Title. II. Series.
PZ7.W65587Ho   [E]   81-70558
ISBN 0-380-80283-X   AACR2

First Camelot Printing, September, 1982

On the edge of the forest in a house full of
dusty recipe books, stringy cobwebs, wispy
brooms, and rusty iron kettles lived the witch
and her child.

The child was totally unpleasant to be around. She was rude, mean, horrible, impossible, and utterly bad. So naturally the witch was very proud of her.

"Isn't she awful?" the witch said. "She's going to be just like me when she grows up."

When the cats closed their slitty eyes and curled up for naps on the dirty floor, the witch child tied their tails together.

"That's a bad girl," her mother said
approvingly. "You're going to grow up to be as
mean as I am."

When her witch aunties sent her nice presents like spiders or empty poison bottles, she never wrote *thank you* letters.

"That's a bad girl," her mother said proudly.
"Everyone is going to hate you as much as they
hate me."

When her mother served dinner, the witch child threw her milk on the floor and stuck out her tongue at the vegetables.

"That's a bad girl," her mother said with a nod.
"You'll get lots of pimples. You're going to be as
ugly as I am."

And because her mother was the dirtiest witch
in the forest the witch child never had to take
baths...

or wash behind her ears...

or change her stockings...

or do the dishes.

She just did whatever she liked. And she didn't do whatever she didn't like.

One day the witch child was outside by the pond, feeding her cat some witchy mud pies.

"Riv–ut, riv–ut, riv–ut," said a voice.

"Stop burping and eat the rest of your mud pie," the witch child said to her cat.

"Meow," said the cat.

"Riv-ut," said another voice.

"Who is saying that stupid word?" said the witch child crossly. "Do you have a frog in your throat?"

"Riv-ha-ha-ha-ha-ut," laughed the voice.

"Where are you?" yelled the witch child. "If you don't show me where you are I'm going to turn you into a frog!"

"Riv-ha-ha-ha-ha-ut," laughed the voice. "You can't turn me into a frog."

"Oh yeah?" said the witch child. "I am the meanest witch child in the forest. And I'm going to grow up to be the meanest witch in the world. You just watch me turn you into a frog."

"You just watch me," said the voice. "I am going to turn you into a pretty little princess. I can perform better magic than witches."

"NO ONE PERFORMS BETTER MAGIC THAN WITCHES!" screamed the witch child. She stood up, covered her eyes with her hands, and spun around seven times.

Then she spoke her magic words:

Friggery, fraggery, fruggery fog,
I now turn you into a little green frog.

And with a whoosh, a green frog hopped to the feet of the witch child.

"Hee, hee, hee," giggled the witch child. "I did it! I turned you into a frog."

"Quick!" said the frog. "Look into the pond."

Still giggling, the witch child kneeled by the pond and saw her reflection smiling back at her.

"You see, my magic is better than yours," said the frog. "You couldn't turn me into a frog because I already was a frog. But I made you smile. And you're as pretty as a princess when you smile."

"But I can't be pretty! I'm a horrible,
impossible, bad witch child!"

"Not any more," said the frog who was always a frog. "Just look," he said, and he hopped off into the forest.

So she did.